I AM READING

Princess Rosa's Winter

JUDY HINDLEY

Illustrated by

MARGARET CHAMBERLAIN

KINGFISHER

First published by Kingfisher 1997
an imprint of Macmillan Children's Books
a division of Macmillan Publishers Limited
20 New Wharf Road, London N1 9RR
Basingstoke and Oxford
Associated companies throughout the world
www.panmacmillan.com

ISBN: 978-0-7534-1038-7

2 4 6 8 9 7 5 3 1
1TR/1108/WKT/(SHOY)/105MA

A CIP catalogue record for this book is available from the British Library.

Printed in China

Contents

Chapter One

It was a winter morning

long ago.

Inside the castle,

it was dark and cold.

When Princess Rosa first woke up,

the candle by her bed

was still alight.

Princess Rosa asked her nurse,

"Why is it so dark

when we wake up?"

Nurse Bonny said to her,

"Because it's winter.

The sun does not get up

till very late, now.

Winter is a dark time."

Nurse Bonny blew on the fire

to make it blaze.

But when the small princess

jumped out of bed,

she still felt cold.

She put on

one gown

over

another –

but she still felt cold!

She said,

"It is too cold, today!

Why is it so cold?"

Nurse Bonny said,

"Because it's winter.

The sun is tired

and the snow is falling.

A dark world is a cold world."

Rosa huddled with her
dogs beside the fire.
Nurse Bonny
toasted bread
and warmed some beer.
Every morning,
breakfast was the same –
but they ate every scrap.

Then they put on their
cloaks and hurried off
to say good morning
to the King and Queen.
Icy breezes whistled
down the hallway.
Cold, white mist
crawled along the
floor.

It was so cold,
the King and Queen
were still in bed.
"Climb up here,
my little climbing Rose!"
the King called out.
"Come and kiss me,
my sweet Rosa!"
cried the Queen.
So she did.
The royal bed had a roof
and curtains.
Inside, it was like a big,
warm cave.
It was very snug.

But here came

the King's Chief Steward

to tell the King

about important business.

And here came

the Lord High Chancellor

to ask the King

a very important question.

And here came the priest

to say a prayer

with the Queen.

And here came her maid

to fix her hair.

And here came the cook
with a big tray of breakfast,
and a little page-boy
with a message.

The doors were guarded
by the royal men-at-arms.
But the cat sneaked past,
and the royal dogs barked,
and finally, the King said,
"Enough!
Everyone must go!"
So they did.

Chapter Two

Off went the princess
and her nurse, and her dogs.
Along the misty hallway,
down a twisty stair.

Out they went
through the great doors
of the castle.
But outside,
big, wet flakes of snow
were falling.

It was too cold
to take the dogs out
for a run.

It was too cold
to take the pony
for a ride.

It was so cold
the falcon
wouldn't fly.

They couldn't even feed

the ducks and fish.

The fish were hidden

underneath the ice.

The ducks and geese and

swans had gone away.

The small princess was cold.

Back they went
through the great doors
of the castle.
It was dinner-time.
Everyone gathered
in the great hall,
and a big fire blazed.
But everyone was gloomy.

For weeks and weeks,

they had not heard

one bit of news,

or one new song

or one new joke.

Everyone was bored.

When dinner came,

they were gloomier than ever.

21

"Same old thing again!"

said Princess Rosa.

"Can't I have an egg?"

"Oh, my darling,

there are no eggs in winter,"

said the Queen.

"When the days are dark,

the hens don't lay them."

The small princess

threw down her spoon.

She cried,

"I don't like winter!"

"Hush!" said Nurse Bonny.

"Winter has some good things."

"Name one,"

said Princess Rosa.

Everyone thought hard.

"I'm sure there are
some good things,"
said the old knight.
"I know!"
cried the little page-boy.
"Snow!
It is good for sleds
and good for sliding,
and it is great for snow-balls."

"Christmas!" said the Queen.

"Christmas is a wonderful winter thing.

We all dress up

and we dress up the castle

with ribbons and little bells

and boughs of greenery and berries.

Then we dance

while the minstrels play for us."

Princess Rosa said,

"Snow is cold.

I don't know if I like it.

I don't know if I like dressing-up

or dancing.

I still think winter is no good."

But the King said,

"There is one good thing

that nobody has mentioned.

Hode."

"What is Hode?"

asked Princess Rosa.

But just then,

CRASH!

The castle doors flew open.

WHOOOO!

The winter wind

came whirling in.

Chapter Three

There in the doorway

stood a huge, white, furry creature.

Everyone went quiet.

The furry creature

marched up

through the hall,

dripping snow.

The wind roared.

The fire crackled.

The drips of melted snow

said, "Hisss!"

The creature kneeled
before the King and Queen,
bowing low.

Then it stood up.

It shook off the snow.

It threw off the bear-skin.

"It's Hode!" cried the King
"It's our wonderful winter visitor."
"It's Hode!" cried the Queen
and the knights
and the men-at-arms.

"It's Hode!" cried the ladies,

and the servants,

and the fiddlers.

"Hurrah!" cried everyone.

"Hurrah!"

Hode was dressed from head to toe

in coloured patches,

and covered from head to toe

with bells and mirrors.

When he moved,

he glinted and he glittered

and he jingled.

From his sleeve

popped a ball

and then another

and another.

Soon, all the balls

were in the air.

He juggled them high

he juggled them low

he juggled them round his arms

and legs

and body.

He whistled them

into his hat

and out his sleeve

and back!

And then he did eleven somersaults
and thirteen back flips.
When he finished,
everyone clapped
and shouted.

"Hurrah!" cried everyone,
"Hurrah!"

The king was so excited,

he could not stop

giving orders.

He cried,

"Bring a bowl of apples!

Bring some walnuts!

Bring some chestnuts!

Bring the fiddles!

Bring some good red wine

for us to drink!

It's time to celebrate!"

"Indeed," said the Queen,

"Why wait for Christmas?"

41

Soon,

everyone was dancing

and all the long, dark winter night
they danced and played.

Very late that night,

when the little princess

went to bed

the snow had stopped.

Her nurse opened the shutter

just a crack

and they peeped out.

The moon was huge and white.

The bright snow gleamed

almost as bright as daylight.

"The snow is beautiful,"

said Princess Rosa.

"And Hode is wonderful,"
she said.

"And dancing is fun!"
she added.

"Ah," said the little princess,

"I can't wait till Christmas!"

About the Author and Illustrator

Judy Hindley lives near an ancient forest in a town built in the time of knights and castles. Judy says, "I like winter because it's one of the best and cosiest times for reading books."

Margaret Chamberlain is interested in how people lived long ago. She says, "Life must have been hard. The seasons really ruled people's lives. But, as Princess Rosa finds out, they also had a lot of fun!"

Tips for Beginner Readers

1. Think about the cover and the title of the book. What do you think it will be about? While you are reading, think about what might happen next and why.

2. As you read, ask yourself if what you're reading makes sense. If it doesn't, try rereading or look at the pictures for clues.

3. If there is a word that you do not know, look carefully at the letters, sounds, and word parts that you do know. Blend the sounds to read the word. Is this a word you know? Does it make sense in the sentence?

4. Think about the characters, where the story takes place, and the problems the characters in the story faced. What are the important ideas in the beginning, middle and end of the story?

5. Ask yourself questions like:
   Did you like the story?
   Why or why not?
   How did the author make it fun to read?
   How well did you understand it?

Maybe you can understand the story better if you read it again!